To those who feel like crying

Tundra Books, an imprint of Penguin Random House Canada Young Readers,
a division of Penguin Random House of Canada Limited

Library and Archives Canada Cataloguing in Publication

Title: If you cry like a fountain / Noemi Vola.
Names: Vola, Noemi, 1993- author, illustrator.
Description: Written by the author in Italian, but not published. First published in English.
Identifiers: Canadiana (print) 20210201924 | Canadiana (ebook) 20210201932
ISBN 9780735270503 (hardcover) | ISBN 9780735270510 (EPUB)
Classification: LCC PZ7.1.V65 Ify 2022 | DDC j853/.92—dc23

Published simultaneously in the United States of America by Tundra Books of Northern New York,
an imprint of Penguin Random House Canada Young Readers,
a division of Penguin Random House of Canada Limited

Library of Congress Control Number: 2021937497

Edited by Peter Phillips
Translated by Debbie Bibo
Designed by John Martz
The artwork in this book was created using markers, pencils, tempera and tears.
The text was set in Albiona Soft.

Printed in China

www.penguinrandomhouse.ca

1 2 3 4 5   26 25 24 23 22

Penguin
Random House
tundra | TUNDRA BOOKS

NOEMI VOLA

Received On

MAY 0 3 2023

Magnolia Library

If you cry like a fountain

tundra

Hey! We can't start the book like this,
with that sad face.

You need to smile, at least at the beginning.
Otherwise everyone will think that you're sad,
and they'll worry.

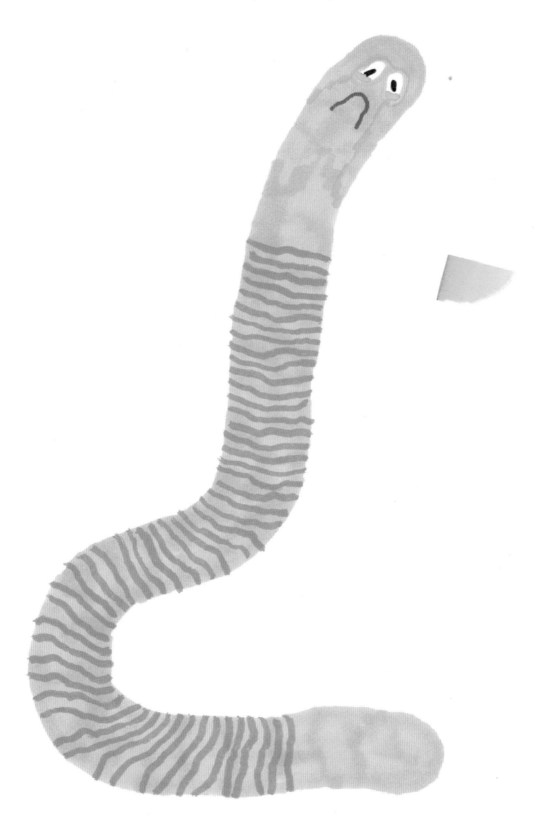

No, come on, please don't cry! Hold back those tears.

Try thinking of something happy in one, two . . .

. . . three!

Oh, no. This is a real disaster.

Hold on a second, or else
you're going to cause a flood!

See what I mean?
If you don't stop, you'll drown!

You might want to wear a life preserver
when you cry.

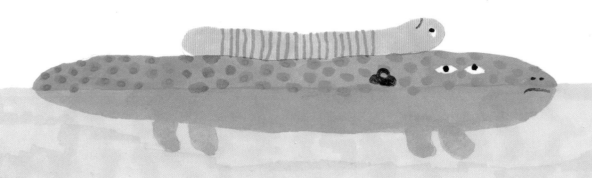

Or you could float on a crocodile and sunbathe
while the sun dries up all your tears.

Do you feel better now?

Good, because there's no use in crying.

Oh, no — what did I say?
What I meant is that there are so many reasons
for crying, but you have to cry better.

Yes! For example, if you cry like a fountain,
you'll be surrounded by friends and
make all the pigeons happy.

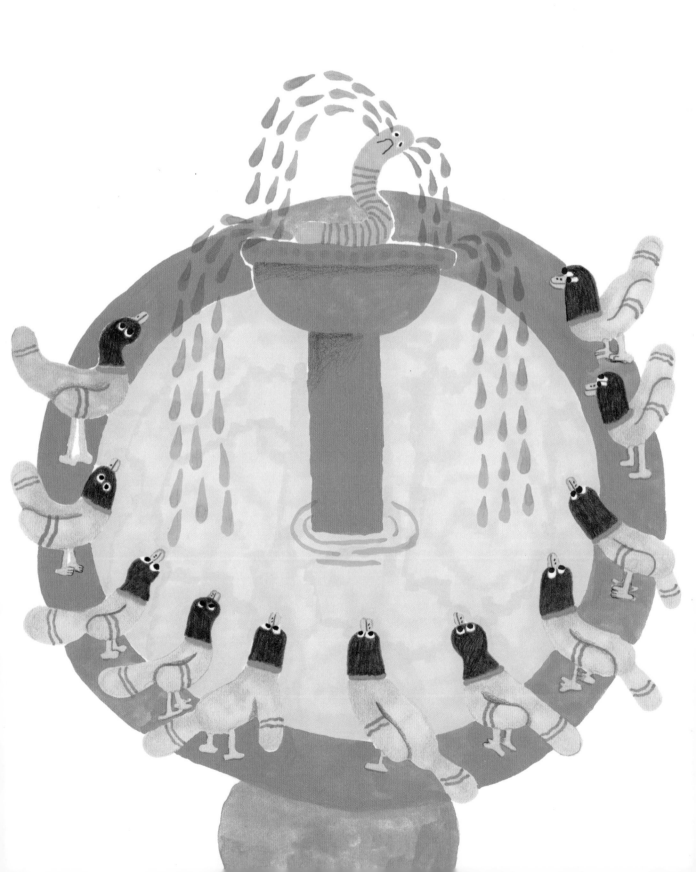

If you feel sad around lunchtime, turn on the stove
and cry until the pot is filled.

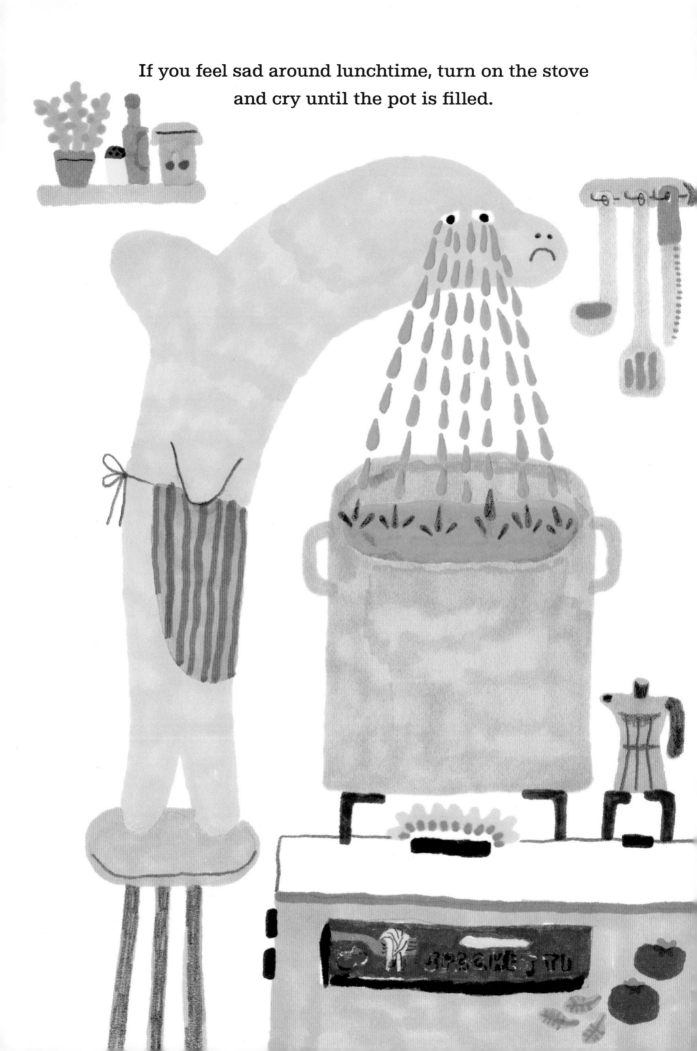

When the tears start to boil, stir in the pasta.
You won't even need to add salt!

If you ever cry in the living room,
just add a little cleaner . . .

and your floors will shine.

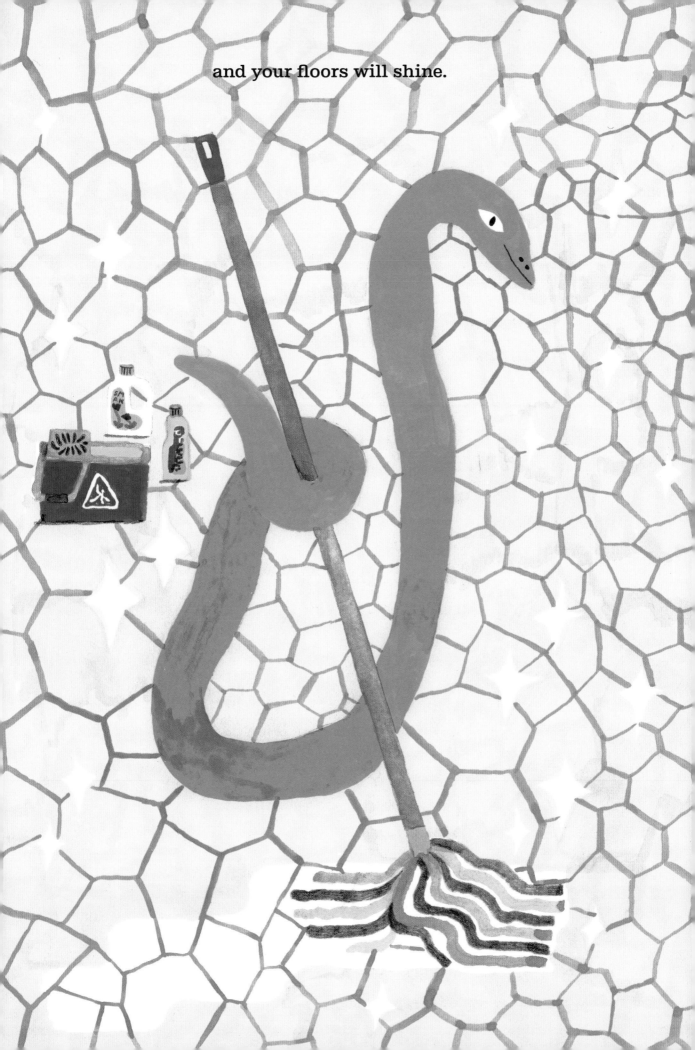

Crying helps improve your
personal hygiene . . .

and your dog's, too.

If that isn't enough,
crying can be done in every season.
If you cry in the winter, you can
skate on your iced tears.

If you cry in the spring,
you can help the
flowers bloom.

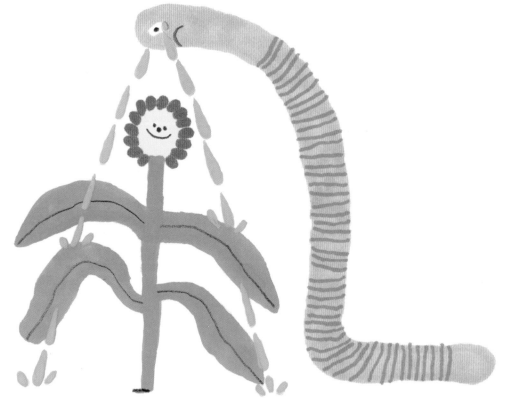

The wonderful thing is that you can cry
on any occasion, even on your birthday.
It's a great way to put out the candles!

Okay, if you aren't convinced yet, check this out: with two cups of tears and one cup of flour, you can make homemade playdough.

And then you can make
surprise presents for
your friends.

HERE IS
A GIFT
FOR YOU.

WOW,
IT'S WONDERFUL!

WHAT
IS
IT?

A
PLAYDOUGH
STATUE OF
ME.

Crying also helps put out small fires.

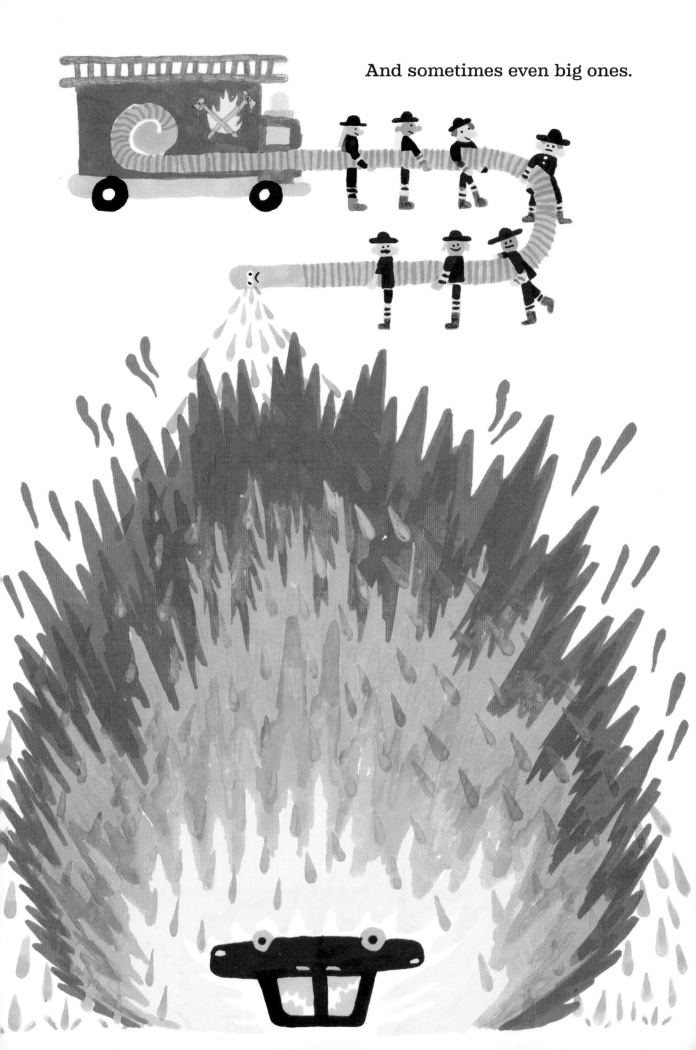

And sometimes even big ones.

Everyone cries:

police officers,

superheroes,

kings,

soccer players,

ants,

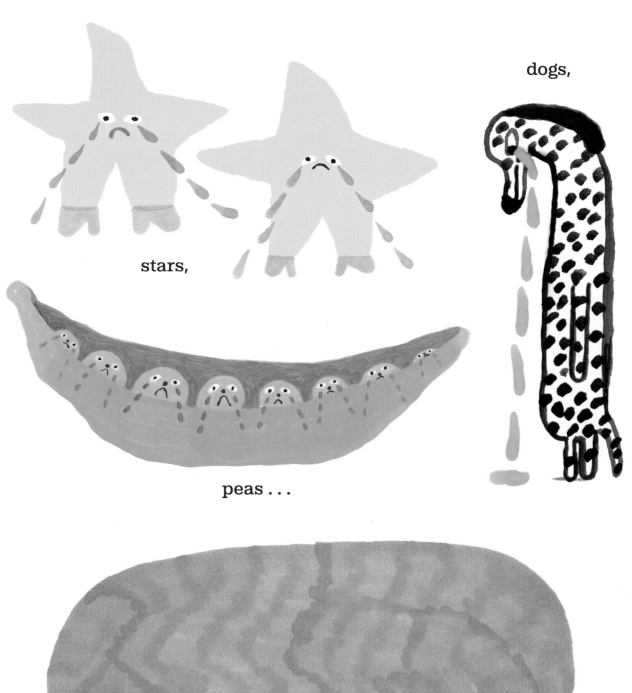

dogs,

stars,

peas . . .

even rocks!

ROCKS?

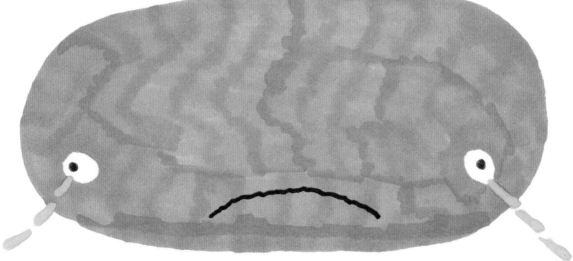

Yes, though no one has ever seen a rock cry
because they are very good at hiding.

There's really no downside to crying.
it's a universal language. It works better than words.

If you ever happen to cry when you're far from home,
don't worry: you'll be understood.

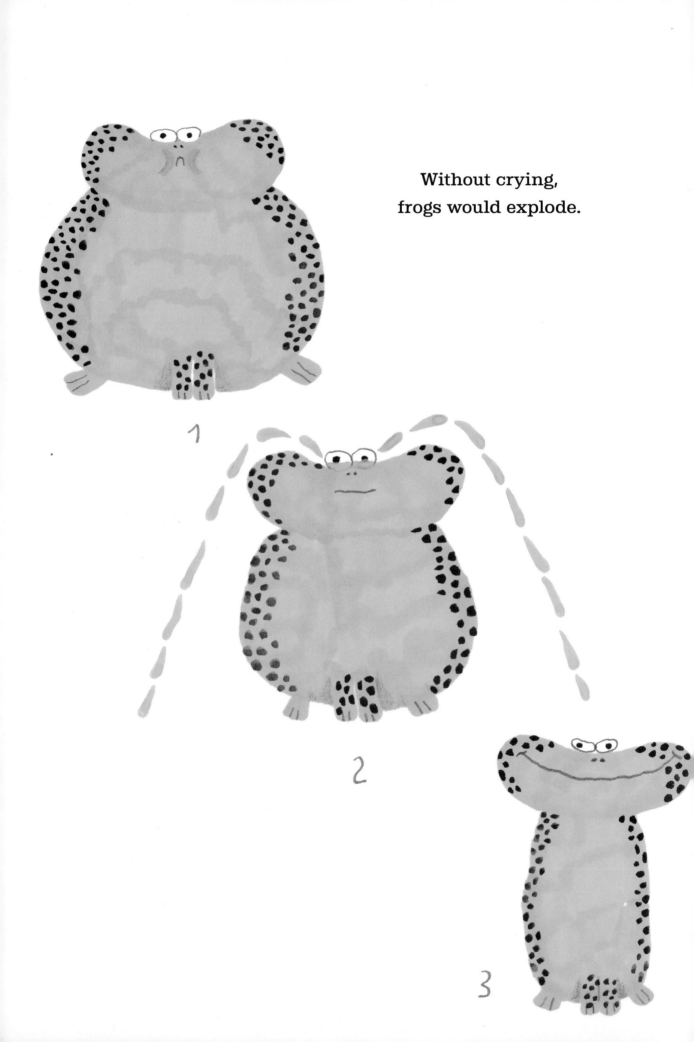

Without crying,
frogs would explode.

Rivers would dry up.

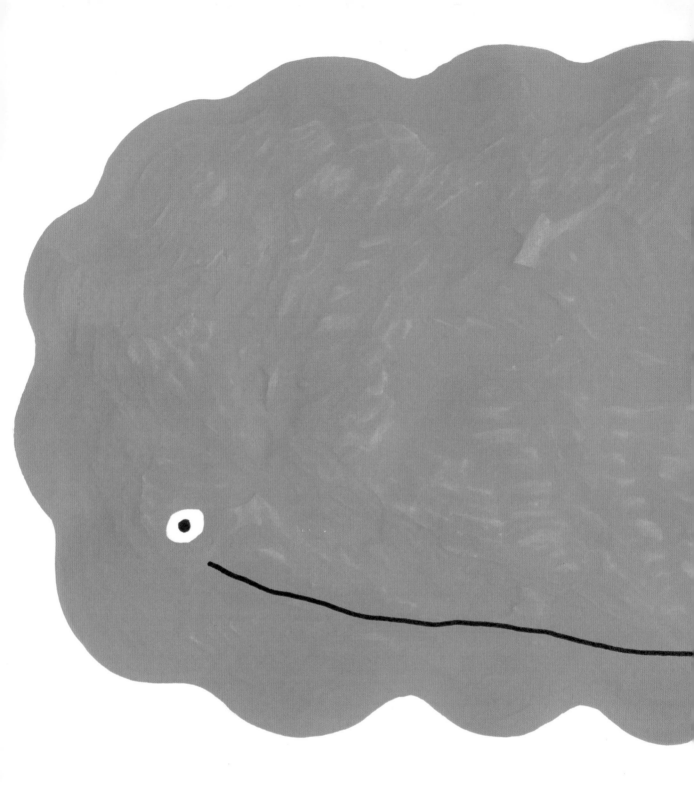

Clouds would keep getting bigger and bigger . . .

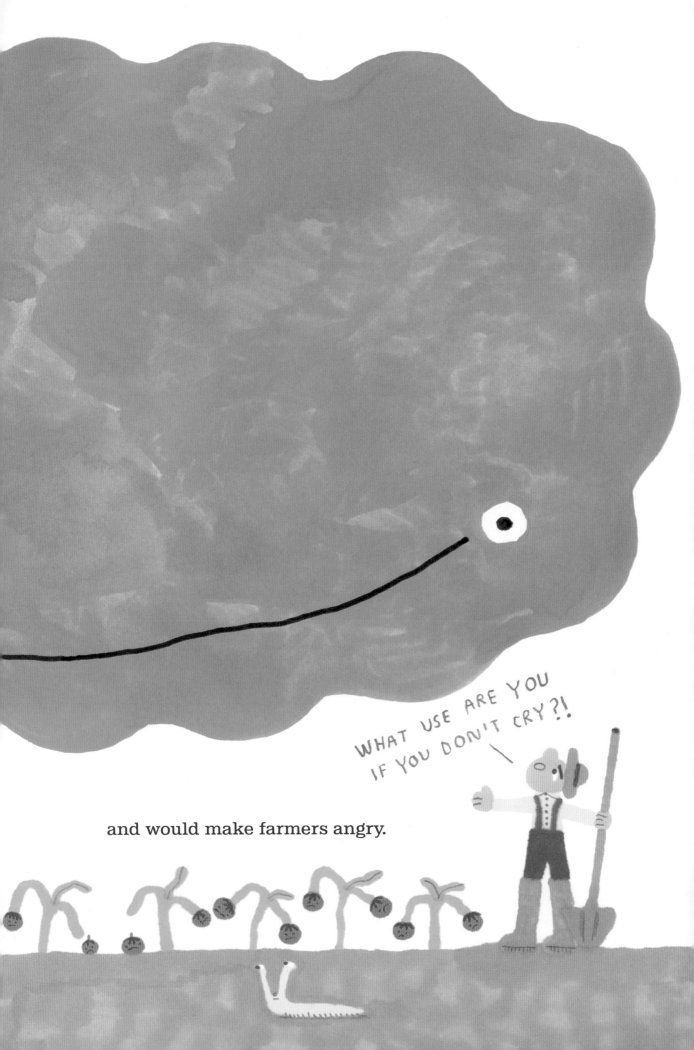

and would make farmers angry.

Crying helps pears grow.

With pears, you can make jam.

Isn't that wonderful?

You're sorry that the book is about to end?
Me too, but don't worry . . . that's life.
Books always end, just like everything else.

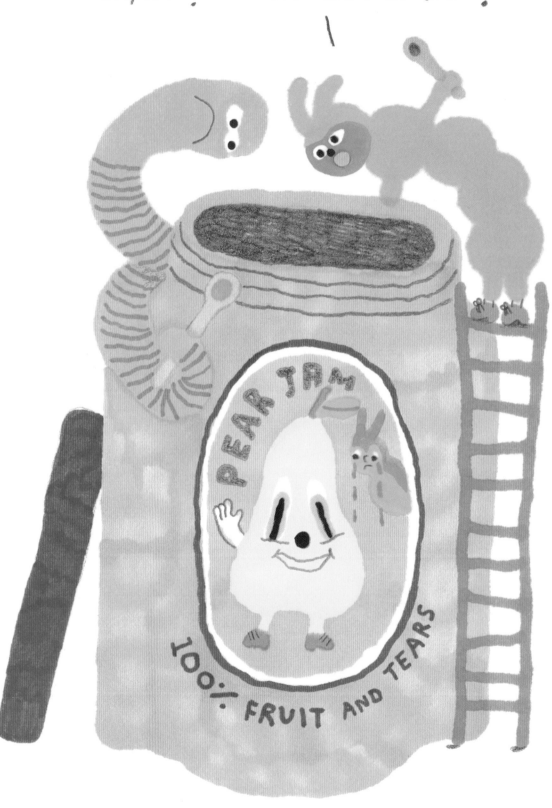

. . . or to swimming pools.